Food Folklore

American Folklore

Children's Folklore
Christmas and Santa Claus Folklore
Contemporary Folklore
Ethnic Folklore
Family Folklore
Firefighters' Folklore
Folk Arts and Crafts
Folk Customs
Folk Dance
Folk Fashion
Folk Festivals
Folk Games
Folk Medicine
Folk Music
Folk Proverbs and Riddles
Folk Religion
Folk Songs
Folk Speech
Folk Tales and Legends
Food Folklore
Regional Folklore

North American Folklore

Food Folklore

BY ELLYN SANNA

Mason Crest Publishers

Mason Crest Publishers Inc.
370 Reed Road
Broomall, Pennsylvania 19008
(866) MCP-BOOK (toll free)
www.masoncrest.com

First printing
1 2 3 4 5 6 7 8 9 10
Library of Congress Cataloging-in-Publication Data on file at the Library of Congress.
ISBN 1-59084-347-9
      1-59084-328-2 (series)

Design by Lori Holland.
Composition by Bytheway Publishing Services, Binghamton, New York.
Cover design by Joe Gilmore.
Printed and bound in the Hashemite Kingdom of Jordan.

Picture credits:
Comstock: pp. 11, 58
Corbis: p. 92
Corel: pp. 29, 31, 36, 38, 50, 55, 59, 62, 72, 76, 85, 100
Digital Stock: pp. 25, 27
Image Ideas: pp. 16, 17
J. Rowe: pp. 8, 10, 20, 44, 52, 54, 64, 65, 78, 80
PhotoDisc: pp. 6, 13, 14, 15, 82, 84, 87, 99
Wildside: p. 89
Cover: "Fall Bounty" by John Atherton © 1943 SEPS: Licensed by Curtis Publishing,
      Indianapolis, IN. www.curtispublishing.com

Contents

Folklore grows from long-ago
seeds. Just as an acorn sends
down roots even as it shoots up
leaves across the sky, folklore is
rooted deeply in the past and
yet still lives and grows today.
It spreads through our modern
world with branches as wide
and sturdy as any oak's;
it grounds us in yesterday even
as it helps us make sense of
both the present and the future.

INTRODUCTION

by Dr. Alan Jabbour

WHAT DO A TALE, a joke, a fiddle tune, a quilt, a jig, a game of jacks, a saint's day procession, a snake fence, and a Halloween costume have in common? Not much, at first glance, but all these forms of human creativity are part of a zone of our cultural life and experience that we sometimes call "folklore."

The word "folklore" means the cultural traditions that are learned and passed along by ordinary people as part of the fabric of their lives and culture. Folklore may be passed along in verbal form, like the urban legend that we hear about from friends who assure us that it really happened to a friend of their cousin. Or it may be tunes or dance steps we pick up on the block, or ways of shaping things to use or admire out of materials readily available to us, like that quilt our aunt made. Often we acquire folklore without even fully realizing where or how we learned it.

Though we might imagine that the word "folklore" refers to cultural traditions from far away or long ago, we actually use and enjoy folklore as part of our own daily lives. It is often ordinary, yet we often remember and prize it because it seems somehow very special. Folklore is culture we share with others in our communities, and we build our identities through the sharing. Our first shared identity is family identity, and family folklore such as shared meals or prayers or songs helps us develop a sense of belonging. But as we grow older we learn to belong to other groups as well. Our identities may be ethnic, religious, occupational, or regional—or all of these, since no one has only one cultural identity. But in every case, the identity is anchored and strengthened by a variety of cultural traditions in which we participate and share with our neighbors. We feel the threads of connection with people we know, but the threads extend far beyond our own immediate communities. In a real sense, they connect us in one way or another to the world.

Folklore possesses features by which we distinguish ourselves from each other. A certain dance step may be African American, or a certain story urban, or a certain hymn Protestant, or a certain food preparation Cajun. Folklore can distinguish us, but at the same time it is one of the best ways we introduce ourselves to each other. We learn about new ethnic groups on the North American landscape by sampling their cuisine, and we enthusiastically adopt musical ideas from other communities. Stories, songs, and visual designs move from group to group, enriching all people in the process. Folklore thus is both a sign of identity, experienced as a special marker of our special groups, and at the same time a cultural coin that is well spent by sharing with others beyond our group boundaries.

Folklore is usually learned informally. Somebody, somewhere, taught us that jump rope rhyme we know, but we may have trouble remembering just where we got it, and it probably wasn't in a book that was assigned as homework. Our world has a domain of formal knowledge, but folklore is a domain of knowledge and culture that is learned by sharing and imitation rather than formal instruction. We can study it formally—that's what we are doing now!—but its natural arena is in the informal, person-to-person fabric of our lives.

Not all culture is folklore. Classical music, art sculpture, or great novels are forms of high art that may contain folklore but are not themselves folklore. Popular music or art may be built on folklore themes and traditions, but it addresses a much wider and more diverse audience than folk music or folk art. But even in the world of popular and mass culture, folklore keeps popping up around the margins. E-mail is not folklore—but an e-mail smile is. And college football is not folklore—but the wave we do at the stadium is.

This series of volumes explores the many faces of folklore throughout the North American continent. By illuminating the many aspects of folklore in our lives, we hope to help readers of the series to appreciate more fully the richness of the cultural fabric they either possess already or can easily encounter as they interact with their North American neighbors.

An ordinary family dinner is a time for talking and sharing.

ONE

A Deeper Meaning
Food as Communication

Folktales use the power of story to illustrate cultural traditions.

ONCE LONG AGO, when times were hard and men wandered the country without homes or jobs, a hungry hobo came to a widow's house and knocked on the door. "Could you spare me any food?" he asked her when she opened the door.

But the widow was a tight-fisted, hard-faced old woman, with a heart that was twisted up like a wad of old newspaper. "My cupboards are bare," she screeched at him and slammed the door in his face.

But the hobo only smiled to himself. He picked up a handful of smooth white stones from the side of the road, and then he knocked again at the old woman's door. When she opened it a crack, he said quickly, "Could I just borrow a pot from you so I can make myself some stone soup?"

The old widow stared at him for a moment, and then she opened the door another inch. "Stone soup? What's that?"

The hobo smiled. "Lend me a pot of water and I'll show you. I'm always happy to share."

The widow squinted at him suspiciously, but she went and got him the pot. Meanwhile, the hobo built a fire by the side of the road, and when the woman returned, he hung the pot of water over the fire. He dropped the white pebbles into the water and stirred them with a stick. "Mmm," he sighed, taking a deep breath of the steam. "This is going to be wonderful soup. Of course, a little piece of meat would make it that much better."

The old woman patted her stomach. "It *is* about lunch time," she admitted. "And I do have a bit of meat I was going to eat. You might as well throw it in the soup."

Like many folktales, stories like "Stone Soup" have been handed down for so long that no one knows anymore where they started. A version of this story has made the rounds in European countries for centuries—and yet John A. Burrison (author of *Storytellers: Folktales and Legends from the South*) found this story being told in Georgia in the 1960s by a man who had heard it from his father, who in turn had heard it from his grandmother—who first told the story as though it were an incident that had happened in her community.

Today, many preschool and elementary classes make stone soup, communicating in a concrete way the power of sharing.

When she had returned with the piece of meat, the hobo chopped it up and added it to his stone soup. "Mmm," he said. "That sure smells good. Of course potatoes add a lot to stone soup."

"I've got a couple of potatoes," the old widow said. She went and got them, and the hobo added them to the pot.

"This is wonderful soup."

He sighed with satisfaction. "Of course, an onion puts the real flavor in stone soup."

And so the old widow brought out an onion, and after that a tomato . . . and then a carrot . . . a little salt . . . and finally a pinch of pepper.

When the soup was cooked, the hobo and the old woman sat

The wheat wafers used during the Communion ritual symbolize the bonds that unite Christians everywhere.

A group of ethnic Russians find that food preparation is a tool for communication within their community. One elder described the importance of their traditional meal-time chores:

> We could never buy a machine to do this work. Then there would be no love between the sisters. Now, if there is a squabble, they are forced to come together and talk it out in the presence of others.

From William B. Moore's "Metaphor and Changing Reality" in Linda K. Brown and Kay Mussell, editors, *Ethnic and Regional Foodways in the United States* (Knoxville: University of Tennessee Press, 1984), p. 97.

down and ate their full. By the time they finished, they were laughing and talking like two old friends.

"Well, I'd best be on my way," the hobo said after he'd helped her wash the dishes.

The old woman looked at the handful of white stones that were still in the bottom of the pot. "Do you want these back?"

The hobo pressed them into her hands. "You keep them. Use them to make stone soup for the next hungry person that comes knocking on your door."

And she did.

At a wedding reception, the bride and groom traditionally feed each other a piece of cake, expressing without words: "We eat from the same cake; we share what we have; we belong to each other."

When families gather around the table, they share an opportunity to make their relationships stronger.

As this story shows, food joins people together. Preparing and sharing a meal does far more than simply provide nourishment for our physical bodies. It acts as a sort of language, a language that sometimes works far better than any spoken or written words. It has the power to knock down the walls between people and bring them close.

Sharing a meal means we gather together around a table; we come close to each other physically, and the act of consuming

Preparing food together is a chance to be close to the people we love.

food becomes an act that both expresses and creates feelings of intimacy. This act may be formal, as when bride, groom, and their guests share a meal at a wedding reception; it may be ritualized, as when Christians take **Communion** or American Hindus participate in a daily religious meal called *prasadam*; or it may be as ordinary and everyday as a family gathering around the dinner table.

Friends may celebrate a work promotion or other achievement with a special meal.

When a newly married couple shares a piece of wedding cake, they express the reality of their union.

At a birthday party, family and friends celebrate by eating a special food—birthday cake. The cake says to the birthday child: "Your life is important to us."

For example, imagine that you and your sister have been fighting all day. Things have become so tense between you that you wish you could stay away from her for the rest of the day; in fact, you think it wouldn't be such a bad idea if you could stay away from her for the rest of your lives! But no, your father calls you both to come and eat, and so there you sit, side by side, glowering at each other. You wish your parents would let you eat at separate times and in separate places. How are you supposed to enjoy your food when your sister keeps bumping you with her elbow every time she takes a bite of mashed potatoes?

You pick up your fork, keeping your arms tight against your sides so you won't touch her, and try to spear a cherry tomato from your salad bowl. Somehow, though, the tomato slips out from under your fork—and plops into your sister's plate, right in the middle of her mashed potatoes.

You're both silent, staring at that tomato. It looks a little like the cherry on top of a sundae. Your sister takes a sip from her glass and snorts, milk dribbling down her face. And then, before you know it, you're both laughing. Somehow, the tension between you starts to ease. Like the old woman in the stone soup story, your angry, twisted-up emotions relax and open. As you finish the meal, you find yourself talking with your sister; you let her back into your heart.

People down through the centuries have understood, often without words, that food offers human beings opportunities for unity and forgiveness. And when we come to the table already in a good mood, food enhances our sense of joy and togetherness. As a result, food has traditionally taken on powerful emotional meanings.

Food can convey many messages. For instance, it can say:

Welcome to our home.

We belong together.

Life is good.

We celebrate your accomplishment.

We forgive you.

It can also communicate what we believe about the meaning of life, about God, and about our place in the scheme of things.

Built on this foundation of deeper meaning, many folk stories and traditions have risen up around food. These traditions vary from region to region; because North America is home to so many cultures, our folk heritage is wide and rich.

In the chapters that follow, we will look at some of the folk stories, customs, and songs that are connected to particular foods. This folklore may seem fanciful or humorous at times—but that's because it's trying to express food's deepest meanings.

And those meanings go far deeper than words.

Corn, beans, and squash were so important to the Iroquois that they saw these foods as three caring sisters.

TWO

From Garden and Orchard
Vegetables and Fruits

JOHNNY APPLESEED.

A 19th-century drawing of Johnny Appleseed, a folk hero who helped "civilize" North America with the apples he planted.

Wh* *HEN EUROPEANS ARRIVED* in North America, they found that some of their seeds grew well in the wild New World—and some did not. The early years in North America were often hard, lean times, as the settlers struggled with a new climate and failed crops.

But Native Americans had an intimate relationship with their continent. They looked on the earth as a beloved mother whom they had lived with and loved for centuries. As a result, they had much to teach the white settlers.

For instance, in northeastern North America, the Iroquois people planted pole beans and squash with corn. They used the strength of the sturdy corn stalks to support the twining beans, while the shade of the spreading squash vines trapped moisture for the growing crop. The Iroquois called these vegetables the "Three Sisters," and they believed that the physical and spiritual well-being of their people relied on the sacred sisters, who were the "sustainers of life," gifts from the Creator. Each crop was protected by one of the Three Sister Spirits, and many folktales were woven around these sisters who would never be apart from one another. They were planted together, eaten together, and celebrated together.

Native American food folklore often expressed Indians' ongoing and practical sense of their dependence upon the earth. As Europeans settled into the new land, they were influenced by these native traditions—but they also created their own food folklore, a folklore that expressed a far different worldview from the Native Americans'. For instance, Paul Bunyan, the Western folk hero famous for his enormous size, ran into a problem one year that was as enormous as he was.

IT all started when Paul planted some corn and squash in his vegetable garden. Before the other corn had even sprouted, one cornstalk was six feet tall—and in two weeks it was as tall as a house and still growing. The same thing happened with one of the squash vines; it grew so fast that people had to keep their windows closed at night. If they didn't, the vine would grow in one window and out the other by morning . . . and the people would have to be cut out of their beds with a knife. When the squash started coming on the vine, people had to be careful, because as the vine continued to grow, the squash would go flying. One man's horse was killed by a flying squash, and half a dozen sturdy barns were smashed.

But the real problem came when the corn and squash roots started soaking up all the water from the ground for miles

> Modern research has found that the Iroquois's companion planting makes good sense scientifically. Not only does the practice conserve moisture in the soil, but the bacterial colonies on the bean roots capture nitrogen from the air, some of which is released into the soil to nourish the high-nitrogen needs of the corn.

around. People's wells went dry; the pinewoods turned yellow; the rivers emptied out; and even the Great Lakes were going down fast. Finally, folks came and told Paul he'd have to get rid of his corn and squash plants.

So Paul hitched up his mighty blue ox Babe and started pulling on the squash vine. Babe had to run all the

Corn was a vital food for early Native Americans—and it soon became equally important to settlers from Europe. Today it continues to be a major ingredient in many North American foods.

way from Michigan to Lake Ontario before he finally managed to pull out that squash plant. Then Paul turned his attention to the cornstalk. He took his ax and made a good deep chip in the stem—but the plant just kept on growing. Finally, he decided he'd have to climb the cornstalk and cut it off from the top. So he hung his ax from his belt and started to climb.

Meanwhile, his friends waited for him down below. They waited . . . and waited . . . and waited. Four days went by, and

NATIVE AMERICAN SQUASH WITH SWEET CORN

One of the new vegetables early settlers encountered in North America was the squash. Native Americans grew countless varieties across the continent—crooknecks in the Northeast, butternuts in the South, and acorn squash in the Northwest. Today the acorn squash continues to be a popular variety.

1–2 cups dried corn
4 medium acorn squash
4 cups of water
white or brown sugar or honey

Add corn to boiling water and cook for 1½ hours or until corn is tender. Peel squash and cut into ¼-inch slices. Add to corn mixture and cook until squash is tender but not falling apart. Add sweetener to taste. Serves 4 to 6 people.

Adapted from Katherine S. Kirlin and Thomas M. Kirlin's *Smithsonian Folklife Cookbook* (Washington, D.C.: Smithsonian Institution Press, 1991), p. 30.

Apples symbolized abundance and health to the early Americans.

they still hadn't seen or heard from Paul. So they all shouted together, "Paul! When you going to take the top off that cornstalk?"

"Hasn't that top come down yet?" Paul hollered back at them. "I cut it off three days ago!"

And that, according to the story, is the truth. The stalk finally stopped growing, the Great Lakes went back to normal, the rivers ran again, and people once more had water in their wells.

Paul Bunyan is a folk hero that first appeared in the 19th century in the oral traditions of the lumberman of Pennsylvania, Wisconsin, French Canada, and the Pacific Northwest. A newspaperman named James MacGillivray made Paul famous by publishing one of his stories in the *Detroit News-Tribune* in 1910. Other professional writers were also inspired by Paul's amazing feats, and Paul Bunyan soon became a national legend. Between 1914 and 1944, a Minnesota advertising man used Paul to promote the products of Red River Lumber Company, and Paul's fame grew still greater.

To the Americans who farmed and lumbered the land, Paul Bunyan symbolized their willingness to work hard to overcome any obstacle nature might set in their way. His huge size and amazing strength spoke of their confidence that they would ultimately win their battle with nature.

As you can see from this story, the European Americans had a very different perspective on their gardens than did the Native Americans. The Indians saw the earth's fruits as honored and well-loved family members—but for white farmers, nature was a dangerous adversary, an opponent to be defeated by their cunning and strength.

But not all American folk heroes had this adversarial relationship with growing things. One hero in particular has come to be seen as almost the

According to Norse myth, the goddess Idun doled out magic apples to the gods; whenever they began to age, their youth would be miraculously restored by eating one of Idun's apples. In an Irish legend, a woman from the otherworld, gives apples to the hero Candle, and they not only nourish him for an entire month, but they also make him immortal.

Beans were once a staple food—and today soy beans are an important crop used in many types of food.

A MIDWEST FOLK TRADITION FOR TELLING THE FUTURE

If you peel an apple without allowing the peeling to break, hold it in your right hand over your head and move it in a circle three times; then drop it over your left shoulder. The letter it forms will be the initial of your future husband.

patron saint of apples, an open-hearted, cheerful fellow who lived in harmony with the earth.

Unlike Paul Bunyan, Johnny Appleseed was an actual historic person. John Chapman was born in 1774 in Massachusetts, and in 1800 he began col-

According to Old World folklore, beans contained the souls of the dead—so if you ate beans, you might become possessed. The old story of "Jack and the Beanstalk" was an example of a bean plant linking our ordinary world with an unknown otherworld. Although wonders might exist in that other realm, it was also considered dangerous to allow an opening between the two worlds (which was why Jack had to chop down the beanstalk).

Apples weren't the only important fruit crop; pears also gave sweetness to North American life.

In the old story of Adam and Eve, the apple represented sin.

lecting apple seeds from cider presses in western Pennsylvania. From these seeds he grew tiny trees, and he took these seedlings with him as he traveled west, planting a string of orchards from the Allegheny Mountains through Ohio and into Indiana. As stories spread about Johnny Appleseed's kindness

Apples were magical, wonderful fruit in the old folklore from Europe—but like beans, in the Old World traditions they carried another darker meaning. After all, the apple symbolized sin and temptation in the biblical story of Adam and Eve. In the old European folk tale of Snow White, made famous by the Grimm brothers, the witch poisons the young girl with an apple, demonstrating that danger and death are hidden beneath the apple's deceptive rosy skin.

But the New World's settlers had a far more cheerful and hopeful outlook on life. They claimed the apple's brighter side and left behind the ancient shadows that lurked around this fruit.

Unlike most vegetables, beans contain protein, and so they offer a nutritious and yet cheap meal. As more and more North Americans were able to afford meat, some people began to associate beans with poverty, and beans again took on negative associations.

toward humanity and his mystical understanding of nature, his character took on a nearly supernatural quality, as though he were one of the ancient saints.

Like many of those saints, he was an odd, half-wild person. According to tradition, his hair was long and ragged, he wore a dented tin pan for a hat and an old coffee sack for a vest, and he carried a tattered Bible under his arm. He gave away thousands of apple seedlings to settlers, and his generosity helped transform the wilderness into a place where white people could more easily find nourishment.

For the European settlers, the apples he brought were powerful symbols of the earth's plenty. When they immigrated to North America, they brought with them a vast body of tradition and folklore that centered on this fruit. In the myths of Scandinavia, the British Isles, and Germany, the apple was a magic thing. There were apples that sang, apples that nourished people for long periods of time, apples that healed, apples that brought fertility, and apples that guaranteed eternal life.

Life was not easy for the settlers on the North American frontier. They worked long and hard for their food; their children were stolen from them by disease and disaster; and an adult's life expectancy was far shorter than it is now. But without a word ever being spoken, apples communicated the promise of ample nourishment, healthy families, and long life. So when Johnny Appleseed spread apples across the land, he was also spreading a sense of hope.

As gardens and orchards were planted across North America, the new Americans mixed their traditions with those of Native Americans. For example, beans in the Old World had been

APPLE PIE RECIPE

Apple pie has gained the reputation as being the most American of desserts. "As all-American as apple pie," people say, linking this favorite pastry with patriotism. But you don't have to be an American to like apple pie. Across both the United States and Canada, apple pie is a traditional favorite. Try your hand at making your own version with this easy recipe.

6 apples

$\frac{1}{2}$ to $\frac{2}{3}$ cup sugar

$\frac{1}{4}$ teaspoon salt

1 teaspoon cinnamon

2 tablespoons flour

1 tablespoon butter

Peel and slice apples. Sift dry ingredients together and combine with apples. Line nine-inch pie shell (you can buy already-made piecrusts) with apple mixture and dot with butter. Cover with top crust. Bake at 450° F for 15 minutes and then reduce temperature to 350°F. and continue baking for an additional 45 minutes.

linked in people's minds with death and decay; they were a vegetable that was not valued as much as other foods. But in the New World, farmers appreciated these plants that grew and matured so quickly. Although European Americans did not worship the bean plant as their "Sister," they did come to connect beans with their new land's productivity. For them beans, like apples, were a symbol of life and prosperity.

This sense of optimism grew in orchards' branches and gardens' vines and stalks. It sustained the hearts of those who sat down to eat meals of succotash and baked beans, apple pie and corn on the cob. Ultimately, it both nourished and symbolized the self-confident spirit of the New World.

Farly North Americans were hunters, but as they cleared the land for farms, meat became more plentiful.

THREE

From Field and Forest,
Sea and Stream
Meat for the Table

Fishermen like this one take their food and livelihood directly from the sea.

LONG AGO, in 1775, the French Acadians were banished by the British from their land in Maine and eastern Canada. Homeless, they wandered for thirty years, until at last they made their way to Louisiana. But they did not go alone on their long trek south. They were accompanied by a loyal sea creature that had become a staple in their diet: the lobster.

Their journey was so long, however, and so exhausting, that the poor lobsters shrunk along the way. By the time they all arrived in the **bayous** and swamps of Louisiana, the lobsters had turned into crawfish. There they settled down and made their homes, imitating their friends, the **Cajun** settlers, by building mud burrows that looked like the settlers' mud chimneys. To this day, they will fight against all odds to survive. Like the Cajuns who eat them, they hold on stubbornly in even the most hopeless situations.

THIS folk story reveals the important role that the crawfish plays not only in the Cajun diet but in the Cajuns' image of themselves. The crawfish continues to be a favorite traditional dish, and "crawfish boils" are common spring events in southern Louisiana. And Cajuns still admire the crawfish's fearless fighting spirit.

Together, humans and sea creatures have thrived in the same region of the continent. Since crawfish are caught directly from the water, their role in the Cajun diet means that people who continue to enjoy this food tradition must live in close connection to the natural environment. In the same way, New England

*In the Cajun legend, big Maine lobsters like this turned into small crawfish as
they traveled to Louisiana.*

fishermen depend on the sea for their livelihood and sustenance. Nature feeds both these groups of people, connecting
them directly and intimately to the earth's water, far more than if
they purchased their food in plastic-wrapped packages.

The folk traditions of Native Americans also recognize a close
interdependence between human beings and the meat they eat.
They honor this interdependence, as we see in the following
story from a tribe in northeastern Canada.

LONG ago when Gluscabi decided to go
hunting, he was angry when the animals in the
woods hid from him. So he went home to the
lodge where he lived with Grandmother Woodchuck. "Grandmother," he said, "make a game
bag for me."

His grandmother made him a game bag

According to Cajun jokes, a crawfish
is so fearless that it will sit on the rail-
road tracks, snapping its claws at an
oncoming train engine.

from woven *caribou* hair, but Gluscabi was not satisfied. "That is not good enough," he said and threw it down.

So Grandmother Woodchuck wove deer hair to make a larger game bag, but again Gluscabi threw it down. "That is not good enough," he told his grandmother.

This time Grandmother Woodchuck took moose hair and wove an even larger bag, but Gluscabi was still not content. "Not good enough," he said again.

"How can I please you?" Grandmother Woodchuck asked. "What do you want?"

Gluscabi gave her a sideways glance and smiled. "Make me a bag out of woodchuck hair, Grandmother."

And Grandmother Woodchuck did as he asked. She pulled the hair from her own belly, and the bag she wove from it was magical. No matter how much you put into it, there would still be room for more. Gluscabi took the bag and smiled. "Thank you, Grandmother," he said. "Now I am happy."

Still smiling his crafty smile, Gluscabi went into the woods and shouted, "Listen, all you animals. A terrible thing is going to happen. The world is going to be destroyed. If you want to escape, you must come and get in my bag where you will be safe."

Just as Louisiana's settlers' were influenced by the food available in their environment, the wealth of seafood available to the New England settlers shaped their folk traditions. New England Yankees are known for their "salty" characters—and some have suggested they owe their tough, practical saltiness to the quantities of dried fish they have eaten over the years.

FOLK TRADITIONS

- In North Carolina, the meat served at community suppers must be from an animal killed within three days before or after a full moon. If this practice is not followed, insist the cooks, the grease will fry out of the flesh, leaving the meat dry and tasteless.
- Only men should cook the meat for large gatherings, and no women should be allowed near until after the meat is sliced. In both North Carolina and Mississippi, women are said to "stop the meat from breathing," which makes the meat tough and bland.
- Across America and Canada, people pair up to tug on the wishbone after a chicken or turkey dinner. Whoever gets the longer piece, gets to make a wish.
- In the islands off the coast of South Carolina, fishermen spit on their bait to guarantee a good catch.
- These fishermen also believe that:

  If the wind comes from the north
  Fish bite like a horse.
  If the wind comes from the south
  Fish bite like a louse.
  If the wind comes from the east
  They bite the least.
  If the wind comes from the west
  They bite the best.

The animals were frightened, and so one by one they climbed into his magic bag. The bag stretched to hold the rabbits and the squirrels, then the raccoons and the foxes, next the deer and the caribou, and finally the bear and the moose. When all the ani-

In the mountains of southeastern America, grazing land was scarce, and many farmers were too poor to own beef cattle. The forest and fields, however, provided tasty alternatives to the animals more commonly used for meat, as this folk song demonstrates.

In come Daddy from the plow,
I want dinner and I want it now:
Ground Hog!

There's some bread up on the shelf,
If you want more, you git it yourself:
Ground Hog!

He picked up his gun and he whistled to his dog,
Off to the woods to catch a ground hog:
Ground Hog!

Daddy returned in an hour and a half,
Had a ground hog as big as a calf:
Ground Hog!

How them children whooped and cried!
Love that ground hog stewed and fried:
Ground Hog!

—Kentucky folk song

mals in the world were inside Gluscabi's game bag, he slung the bag over his shoulder and went home laughing.

"Grandmother," he called, "now we never have to spend our time hunting for food. Whenever we want meat to eat, we can reach into my game bag."

Grandmother Woodchuck shook her head. "Gluscabi, the animals will sicken and die inside your bag. Then there will be none left for your children and for their children. Hunting is good for you, and it is good for the animals. It keeps you both strong."

Gluscabi heard what his grandmother said. He took the animals back into the woods and let them go. "The world was destroyed," he told them, "but I put it back together."

FOOD traditions and customs tell a lot about the way people see the world and their place in it. Cajuns saw their own reflection in the particular meat they ate. Native Americans realized that greed for meat could damage the earth's balance. And early African Americans understood they would need all their wits if they wanted to put meat on their table.

In slavery's world, generosity and cruelty

The trickster Brer Rabbit was a popular character in many African American folktales.

Most people today do not think of frogs as a source of meat—but some still consider them a delicacy.

African Americans were not the only ones to enjoy eating frogs. French Canadians still consider them to be a delicacy.

There once was a frog who lived in a bog
And played a fiddle in the middle of a puddle.
What a muddle!
Better go 'round. Better go 'round.

His music was short for soon he was caught
And now in the middle of a griddle is frying
And he's crying:
"Rather be drowned. Rather be drowned."

—Canadian folk song

were often mixed together in unpredictable ways. African Americans were forced to protect their power, intelligence, and dignity by hiding it from the eyes of white people. Perhaps that's why African American folktales are filled with sly tricksters who win out against the odds.

For instance, one day Brer Coon was all upset because he had no meat in his house. He had tried catching some frogs, but the frogs were too fast and too smart. Now his children were hungry and his wife was so angry with him that she beat him over the head with a broom. But his friend Brer Rabbit gave him some help.

Brer Rabbit told Brer Coon to stretch out beside the river as though he were dead. The sun shone on him, the flies landed on him, and he never moved. Then Brer Rabbit shouted into the water, "Hey, Old Coon is dead."

A big old frog croaked back, "I don't believe it, I don't believe it, I don't believe it." And all the little frogs chimed in. "I don't believe it, I don't believe it, I don't believe it."

Brer Rabbit said, "I tell you what, why don't you dig a big hole where we can bury him? Then you'll know he's dead."

So the frogs began to dig, and Brer Rabbit lay down to take a little nap. When he woke up, he asked, "Is that hole deep enough yet?"

"Deep enough, deep enough, deep enough," the frogs croaked.

In the woods of South Carolina, a region where people once relied on small wild animals for their meat, this folk song described a vision of paradise.

Now our troubles have ended
How happy we will be.
A thousand trees surrounding us,
And a possum in every tree.

Opossums look like large rats—and most people don't find them very appetizing. When food is short, though, you'll eat most anything. Besides, they're said to taste like chicken.

"Can you jump out?"

"Believe we can, believe we can, believe we can."

"Then it's not deep enough yet," said Brer Rabbit. "You'd better keep digging."

So the frogs dug some more, and Brer Rabbit took another nap. This time when he woke up, he asked the frogs again, "Can you jump out?"

"No we can't, no we can't, no we can't," they sang.

Brer Rabbit let out a shout. "Rise up, Brer Coon, and get your meat!"

And that night Brer Coon and all his family ate meat for their supper.

When the Spanish settled the Southwest, they introduced livestock to the Native Americans and changed the native diet forever. Not only could Native Americans now eat more meat; for the first time, they also had dairy products and lard for frying foods.

MANY North Americans, however, would not be happy to serve Brer Coon's frogs on their tables. As the white colonists settled down and established farms, fewer of them depended on hunting and fishing. Instead, they raised their meat.

Still, when food is scarce, people are not so picky about what they eat. Families who had little considered chicken to be the ultimate in feasting, a dish reserved for Sunday dinners and special occasions. The rest of the time they ate whatever meat they could—including animals like woodchuck and possums. On butchering day, they wasted nothing; every possible part of a cow or pig was valued as food.

Gradually meat, and especially beef, became a symbol of prestige. Those who could eat steak and other cuts of beef had far more social and financial power than those who ate off the land. People who ate organ meats, pigs' feet and ears, and other "less desirable" parts of an animal's body, were often seen as primitive, uncouth, perhaps even disgusting.

People who followed folk traditions, however, prided themselves on putting to good use every edible piece of meat. African Americans were said to eat all of the pig "except the squeal," and Italian American immigrants ate not only pigs' feet, ears, and skin, but lambs' heads as well. (The dish is still an Easter delicacy among some Italian families.) Like Native Americans in the West who used the entire body of the bison they hunted, butchering and eating traditions from these ethnic groups let nothing go to waste.

If you eat the entire animal, you cannot disguise the fact that you are in fact eating a once-living creature. Your connection to the beasts of

Hispanic Americans continue to make good culinary use of the entire animal's body. One dish, called *menudo,* is made from tripe (the stomach lining of a cow's stomach) and cow's or pig's feet. In southern Texas, this soup is sometimes called "bone coffee." Served with tortillas and plenty of chili, menudo is thought to be both fortifying and healing.

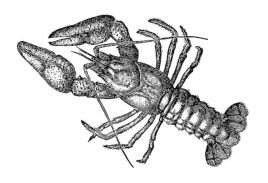

field, forest, and water becomes obvious. In a way, you honor the animal's life by valuing each part of its body as nourishment.

Contemporary North American food traditions, though they prize meat as a main dish in nearly every meal, avoid the knowledge that meat is animal flesh. Most of us do not think of roast beef as cow muscle; instead, we buy our cuts of meat at the grocery store— neat, sanitary, and wrapped in plastic.

Sometimes we forget the many folk traditions that express our dependence on the earth around us. Like Gluscabi in the Native American folktale, our search for convenience may in fact eventually damage the earth. (Acres of rain forest in South America have been cut down so that beef can be raised for North Americans' consumption.)

But our heritage of food folklore reminds us that grocery stores are only convenient way stations that bring our meat to us. Each time we go out for a hamburger or fried clams; each time we gather around the dinner table for a meal of chicken, pork chops, or fish; each time we enjoy a holiday feast of turkey or ham, we are really eating from nature's plate.

In various shapes and forms, bread is an essential food across North America.

FOUR

Daily Bread
Wheat, Corn, and Other Grains

A talking pancake may seem silly—but it illustrates the important role breadstuffs played in people's lives.

PAUL BUNYAN didn't just grow enormous corn and squash plants. He also grew enough wheat to supply his crew of lumberman with flapjacks every morning.

These flapjacks weren't ordinary pancakes either. They were cooked on a griddle that was so large you couldn't see across it when the smoke was thick. Sourdough Sam, Paul's cook, had fifty men with pork rinds tied to their feet go skating across that griddle every morning to grease it. The batter was mixed in huge barrels, and a man had to be pretty strong just to flip those immense pancakes, let alone carry them to the table.

LIKE the other Paul Bunyan folktales, this story demonstrates America's spirit of brash confidence. Everything was big in the New World—and men were the conquerors who feasted off the continent's immense offerings.

But when the settlers first arrived from Europe, they told different stories about pancakes.

For example, once upon a time there was a good housewife who had seven hungry children. One day she began to fry them up a batch of pancakes made from good wheat flour. All the children gathered around to watch.

"Oh, give me a bit of pancake, Mother," said the first child.

"I am so hungry!" said the second child.

"Oh, do give us a bit of pancake!" said the third.

"Oh, do, kind mother!" said the fourth.

"Oh, do!" said the fifth.

"Oh, do!" said the sixth.

"Oh, do!" said the seventh. "We want to eat that pancake up!"

When the pancake heard their voices, it became frightened, for it knew it was about to be devoured by seven hungry children. It leapt out of the pan and rolled right out the door.

The children screamed and ran after it, their mother following behind them with the griddle in her hand. But the pancake kept on rolling.

It met a man, who called out to it, "Dear pancake, don't roll so fast. Wait a bit and let me eat you."

"Oh, no," said the pancake. "I have just escaped seven hungry children, and you won't catch me." And it rolled on like a wheel down the road.

Along its way it met Henny Penny, Cocky Locky, and Ducky Lucky, but none of them could catch the pancake. When it had rolled for a long time, it met Piggy Wiggy.

"Good day, pancake," said the pig.

"Good day," shouted the pancake and rolled even faster.

"Wait a bit," said the pig. "Don't be in such a hurry-scurry. We can walk together and keep each other company. These woods are dangerous, you know, and you'll be far safer with me."

So they walked together until they came to a river. "Sit on my snout," the pig said, "and I will carry you across the water."

So the pancake did—and gulp! the pig swallowed it in one bite.

THIS story was told by the settlers who came from Norway. Those who came from Germany told a similar folktale, and in

This folk song, sung and played at square dances in Texas during the 19th century, shows the importance of both wheat (biscuits) and cornbread in the American west.

Meet your partner, pat her on the head,
If she don't like biscuit, feed her corn-bread.
Roll on, doughboy, roll your dough,
Roll on, doughboy, roll your dough.

With the arrival of European settlers in the New World, wheat replaced corn as the most important crop.

both stories, the wheat pancake escapes the hungry children, only to be eaten by the clever pig. In one version of the story, however, the pancake has mercy on the hungry children and at last sacrifices itself to fill their empty stomachs.

Pancakes and other foods made from flour were the staples of every household; even the poorest family usually had bread. But in the food folklore of the Old World, even this most dependable of foods was all too likely to get away from the hungry family.

But folktales spread from land to land and culture to culture. As they are assimilated into new surroundings, the stories change to match their environments. In the New World, for instance, the hardy settlers of the eastern mountains told this same story—but

Early cultures saw that grain "died," was buried in the ground, and then sprouted into new life once again. To them it seemed like the most fundamental and hopeful of all magic spells, a promise that each human creature will also live eternally.

According to Greek tradition, the goddess Demeter taught human beings how to tame nature by growing grain. However, when Demeter's daughter Persephone was stolen by Hades, the god of the dead, the world lay cold and barren, and no grain could grow. Demeter struck a bargain with Hades and convinced him to allow Persephone to return to the earth for a part of each year. This arrangement mirrors grain's growing cycle.

Interestingly, the Iroquois told a very similar story. According to their tradition, the Corn Goddess married a human man, bringing with her the gift of corn. When she left him to go back to the other world, cold came to the earth and the grains dropped from the ears of corn. Lonely for his wife and desperate to feed his people, the Corn Goddess's husband followed her. Although she would not go back with him, she gave him a gift: corn kernels that would grow for half the year, when the earth was warm.

now the fleeing pancake became a gingerbread boy. No longer a necessary staple to feed hungry children, the hero of the story was baked by an old woman longing for a child.

African Americans also made this story a part of their folklore—but in their version the wheat pancake was a corn johnny-cake. Wheat had been the Old World's primary grain, but in North America, corn was the staple.

When the white settlers arrived in the New World, they found the Native Americans eating this large-kernelled grain. Indians often saw corn, or maize, as the symbol of all life, and many tribes worshiped the corn goddess, the giver of life and sustenance. For the Native Americans, corn meant fertility, happiness, plenty. They depended on maize for their survival, and stories about its origin and life cycle permeated their lives. For them, corn was a gift from the eternal world of the Great Spirit.

Nutritionists today advise making carbohydrates—the nutrient found in grain products—a major part of our diets. The "food pyramid" puts these foods as the foundation to the rest of the pyramid, the largest layer of the triangle.

SOUTHERN CORN BREAD

2 cups cornmeal
¼ cup flour
3 tsps baking powder
1 tsp salt
¼ tsp baking soda
2 egg yolks
1½ cups milk
2 tbsps melted shortening

Mix ingredients together and pour into a greased frying pan. Bake at 450 degrees for 25 to 30 minutes.

Adapted from editors Katherine S. Kirlin and Thomas M. Kirlin's *Smithsonia Folklife Cookbook* (Washington, D.C.: Smithsonian Institution Press, 1991), p. 157.

Bread is important to the religious ceremonies of many faiths. This is a loaf of challah, a Jewish bread used to celebrate the Sabbath and holidays.

Long-ago cultures depended on hunting and gathering for their food. Today our food is harvested by big machines, processed at factories, and sent to supermarkets—but we still depend on the earth for sustenance.

Europeans were at first reluctant to accept corn as grain. Although they ate it as a vegetable, as we still do today, they believed as a grain, corn was far inferior to wheat. For the Spanish settlers in the American West, the wheat-corn controversy even became a religious dilemma.

The Spanish liked breads baked with wheat flour, the kind they had eaten at home—and the Catholic Church considered wheat the only acceptable grain for Communion wafers. Because the natives had revered corn for centuries, however, they turned up their noses at this strange white flour. For them, wheat bread wasn't real food. The Spanish couldn't even give wheat bread away to beggars, so it was no wonder that Native Americans were reluctant to accept that Communion's bit of wheat bread was sacred. Eventually, however, as the Hispanic colonists planted wheat fields, the Indians who tended them were forced to eat the bread they received as wages. The Native Americans of the West began to make their **tamales** and **tortillas** from wheat flour as well as corn—and many of them also converted to Catholicism and accepted wheat Communion wafers.

Meanwhile, the people in the South continued to eat cornmeal bread, but across North America acres of wheat and other grains were planted. The central part of North America became one of the world's "bread baskets."

For all early cultures, bread was the most important of all foods. Because bread making involved grain—of one sort or another—which died and was resurrected with the seasons, bread came to represent life with all its cycles of death and rebirth. These early cultures believed that when they ate bread, they were eating the body of a god who died and then was resurrected to new life. This tradition is still a vital part of the Christian world today, where the Communion bread symbolizes the life, death, and resurrection of Jesus Christ.

Each time we take a bite of bread we may not consciously make the connection to this long heritage of symbolism and meaning. But bread continues to be a staple in our diets.

As Italian immigrants have been absorbed into North American culture, we have also come to love another grain food— pasta. Traditionally, North Americans have made meat their main dish at any meal, but pasta allows a grain product to become the meal's central food.

When early cultures began growing grain, it marked the line between one way of life and another. Once human beings depended on hunting and gathering for their food—but now they became farmers. Grain transformed the way people looked at the world. Today, whether in bread, tortillas, pasta, or a bowl of breakfast cereal, grain continues to supply us all with life and nourishment.

Sugar is one of the most common and oldest of flavorings. Some of today's sugar comes from sugar beets.

FIVE

The Spice of Life
Flavorings and Seasonings

Salt was seen as such an essential ingredient for food that folktales compared it to the love between a daughter and her father.

ONCE THERE WAS a king who had three daughters. One day, as they were sitting around the table, he asked them, "How much do you love me?"

The oldest one said, "Father, I love you as much as my eyes."

The second one said, "I love you as much as my heart."

And the youngest answered, "I love you as much as salt."

"What!" the king cried. "You only love me as much as salt?" He flew into a rage and had the youngest daughter banished from the castle.

Sadly, the rejected daughter went out into the world to make her way. An innkeeper took her in and taught her cooking skills. As time went by, she became famous for her delicious cooking.

When the king heard of this new and skillful cook, he hired her to make the court's food, not realizing she was his own daughter. Her first task was to prepare the wedding feast for the oldest daughter's wedding.

On the wedding day, everyone praised the elegant dishes. When the king's favorite dish arrived, he smiled and took a taste—and then he threw down his fork in disgust. "This has not been salted! Have the cook brought to me!"

When the cook entered the hall, her head high, the king snapped at her, "You careless girl, you have forgotten to salt my favorite food."

The cook answered, "You drove away your youngest daughter because she said she loved you as much as salt. Perhaps now you can see her love was not so small. After all, what is food without salt? And what is life without love?"

When the king heard these words, he recognized his daughter, and he hung his head in shame. He begged her forgiveness, and then with open arms, he welcomed her back to her rightful place at his side.

NORTH America's earliest European settlers brought this folktale with them. The ancient story has roots in England, Germany, Austria, Italy, and as far away as India. William Shakespeare even included a version of the tale in one of his plays, *King Lear*. The story says something about a daughter's love—but it also clearly indicates that the food we've already discussed—fruit and vegetables, meat, and grains—are all very good, but without seasoning, eating would not be nearly such a pleasurable experience. And of course the most common of spices is salt.

FOLK TRADITIONS

- The devil often lurks behind your left shoulder—but if you throw salt over that shoulder, you will chase him away and thus ward off evil.
- If you spill salt, you will have bad luck.

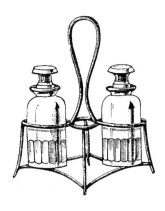

According to ancient folk traditions, all matter contained salt. What's more, salt had the ability to penetrate and preserve other food. People associated it with life, with the soul, and with immortality. A folktale told by Chinese Americans tells how a *phoenix* (another emblem of eternal life) brought salt to humanity, and

According to a Chinese folktale, salt came from a phoenix's flame.

Christians remember that Jesus called his followers the "salt of the earth," referring in part to their power to spread life throughout the entire world despite their small numbers. According to **medieval** traditions, salt had the power to ward off evil, and it was used in both magic spells and religious rituals.

Until the coming of the white man, however, Native Americans did not use salt as a seasoning. Instead, for the Northeastern tribes, maple sugar was often their only spice. This sweet flavoring was an essential part not only of their foods but of their stories and celebrations as well.

The Ojibwa people tell the story of Ininatig, the "man tree" who gave his "blood" to save the people when they were starving at the end of one long and desperately harsh winter. Because Ininatig gave them the strength they needed to survive, the Ojibwa continue to honor the tree spirit's generosity. Each spring they hold maple festivals that are both celebrations and thanksgiving offerings.

When Europeans settled the New World, they too learned to tap the maple tree for its sweet sap. They also continued to depend on sugar from sugarcane, imported from the West Indies. Sweet foods were far less common in colonial days than they are now, and sugar and sweets were rare treats to be treasured. Be-

Sugarcane from the West Indies was important to North America's early economy—and sugar was a treasured commodity. Unfortunately, the sugarcane industry was closely linked to slavery.

THE MEANINGS OF HERB AND SPICES

Herbs come from a plant's leaves or stems; spices come from the seeds or bark. According to folklore, these ingredients not only added flavor; they also had great emotional and spiritual power. Here are the traditional meanings for some common herbs and spices.

Basil: royalty
Betony: protection against witchcraft
Caraway: protection against witchcraft; the power to bring home wanderers; an ingredient in love potions
Carnation (also called "gillyflower"): comfort for the heart
Cinnamon: holiness (cinnamon was once more valuable than gold)
Coriander: love
Dill: good fortune
Fennel: courage; prolonged youth; protection against evil
Ginger: protection against disease
Hyssop: purity and cleansing
Lemon balm: comfort for melancholy
Oregano: joy
Rosemary: fidelity, abiding love and friendship, the power of memory
Rue: repentance
Sage: salvation, long memory, wisdom
Tansy: life eternal
Thyme: courage; protection against nightmares

A SOUTHERN FOLK SONG

Little bird, little bird, go through my window,
And buy molasses candy.
Go through my window, my sugar lump,
And buy molasses candy.

Molasses is the thick brown syrup that is separated from
the raw sugar during sugar manufacture. As a sugar
byproduct, it was cheaper and more readily available to
early North Americans.

cause sugar was so highly prized, it became connected in people's
minds with both love and luxury.

The Anishinabe people of the Great Lakes Region tell another
folktale about sugar. According to this story, maple syrup once
dripped directly from every broken twig of a maple tree. The wa-
tery sap did not have to be collected and boiled down, and so
people would simply lie on their backs beneath the trees, their
mouths open, growing fatter and lazier as they sucked down the
delicious syrup. When the Great Spirit saw what had happened,
he took buckets of water and added them to the maple trees'
veins, thinning the sap so that it was now barely sweet. He also
made the sap only run in the springtime rather than all year long.
"Good things must be enjoyed in small quantities," he said, "or
the people will suffer."

Perhaps our world today could profit from this warning! We
still value sweet foods, just as earlier North Americans did, but

now sugar and sugar products are more readily available than they once were; many packaged foods have high sugar contents as well. Scientists warn that North Americans consume far more sugar than is healthy; since sugar is high in calories and low in nutrients, many people who consume too much sugar struggle with weight problems and health conditions brought on by obesity. As our environment changes, our food traditions adapt as well. When a once-rare food becomes convenient and easy to obtain, good health demands that we find a new balance in our eating habits.

Sugar and salt are probably the most ancient of spices, but pepper comes in third place. Europeans had been using pepper since about the fifth or sixth century BC, and they believed it not only added flavor to bland foods but also had the power to heal diseases. In the centuries before refrigeration, people in warm climates also depended on pepper to mask the taste of meat beginning to go bad.

When Europeans arrived in the Southwest, they discovered an alternative to black pepper—chili peppers. The native tribes there had been growing chili for more than 8,000 years. One story from the Zuñi Pueblo people tells of the chili pepper's origin.

According to a Chinese American folk tradition, sugarcane protects against evil and brings a home wealth and harmony. Some families place stalks of sugarcane beside doors to both ward off evil spirits and welcome the God of Wealth. Sugarcane is used as a decoration during marriage ceremonies and at New Year's celebrations to ensure joy and prosperity in the days to come.

European settlers brought with them a long tradition regarding the importance of pepper. During the Middle Ages it was used as a substitute for money when paying rents and ransoms. It was such a valuable commodity that in the 15th century it inspired the Portuguese mariners' dangerous voyages to the east and eventually to the New World.

Chili peppers come in many shapes, colors, and sizes.

THE Twin War Gods were two mischievous boys who stole the rain gods' thunder and lightning. As they played with their powerful new toys, violent storms descended on their heads. Rain poured down and flooded their home, drowning their old grandmother. She was so angry with the twins for their foolish carelessness that from her grave grew fiery pepper plants. The Twin War Gods plucked the pepper plants from the ground and sowed the seeds across the land. According to folk tradition, this explains why today there are more than 1,600 varieties of chili peppers growing across the Southwest and down into South America.

BESIDES salt, sugar, and pepper, North American settlers used many plants as flavorings for their foods. Two of the most

GARLIC FOLKLORE AND HISTORY

- During the Plague in Europe's Middle Ages, garlic may have protected some people from theworst of the disease.
- During colonial times, garlic cloves were bound to the feet of smallpox victims and placed in the shoes of whooping cough sufferers.
- Garlic has been used to treat intestinal worms since ancient times.
- The Prophet Mohammed recommended garlic as a cure for snake and scorpion bites.
- Roman nobility avoided garlic, but it was included in soldiers' rations to make them strong. Egyptian slave masters fed garlic to their laborers to improve their strength.
- Folk medicine claims that garlic improves the voice, the complexion, and the intellect, while it also helps broken bones to heal.
- In World War I, garlic was used as an antiseptic in poultices.

ONION MEDICINE

- A syrup made from the juice of one onion, mixed with honey, alleviates congestion from colds or the flu.
- A roasted onion is sometimes used as a poultice for earaches.
- An onion a day is said to prevent hair loss.
- Onion juice may work as a cure for athlete's foot.
- Modern cardiologists have found that a daily onion lowers cholesterol. Both garlic and onions have also been found to lower blood pressure, help prevent blood clots, and reduce the chances of stomach cancer.

common of these were onions and garlic. Not only did these plants make food more tasty; they also, according to folk tradition, had the power to heal and ward off evil. Other plants—the herbs and spices that add sharper tastes to meat and vegetable dishes—shared similar powers with the onion and its cousin garlic.

According to these folk beliefs, the individual consumption of food was not merely a matter of personal taste; it had more far-reaching implications. Herbs and spices, products of the natural world, were gifts from the otherworld, and so they had the power to connect human beings with eternity. This power could be both beneficial and dangerous; it could heal and it could kill. Some flavorings became ingredients in magic rituals (like garlic, which was thought to be a power-

ful spell against vampires and witches), others took on sacred significance, and still others were valued for their medicinal value. Today, researchers have found that many of these herbs and spices do in fact have healing properties.

When we shake salt or pepper on our food, enjoy a cinnamon-and-spice cookie, or savor a garlicky tomato sauce, we do not think of a deeper significance beyond the pleasure of good food. But our folklore heritage reminds us that spice has meaning. These flavorings testify to the earth's power to heal and nurture, and they hint at life's deepest and most lasting joys.

For today's North Americans, the hamburger is an important cultural food.

SIX

The Ties That Bind
Food as a Symbol of Group Identity

Many Native Americans have folktales that explain corn as a gift from the spiritual world.

ONCE THERE WAS a Cherokee boy who lived with his grandmother. Every day when he came home from hunting, his grandmother would go into their storehouse and come back with a basket of corn to cook with the game he had caught. One morning, however, the boy looked into the storehouse and found that it was empty—and yet when he returned that night, his grandmother went into the storehouse as usual and came back with a basket of corn just as she always did.

"That's strange," he said to himself. The next day he hid and watched through a crack in the storehouse wall to see where his grandmother was getting the corn.

As he watched, his grandmother set her basket down in the middle of the empty storehouse. Then she bent over it as she rubbed her hand over the side of her body. Dried corn poured out of her side and filled the basket.

The boy was terrified by what he had seen. When his grandmother came out and saw his face, she shook her head sadly. "Now that you know my secret," she said, "I cannot live with you as I did before. Before the sun rises tomorrow I will be dead. Do as I tell you, though, and you will always be able to feed yourself and your people. I will be gone, and yet I will never leave you." In a tired whisper, the old woman instructed the boy to plant her body in the ground. Then she told him how to tend the earth and cultivate the new life that would grow from her grave.

In the morning, the old woman was dead, just as she had predicted. With tears in his eyes, the boy did as she had told him to do. As the corn stalks grew tall from her grave, he could still hear

her whispering to him as the wind stirred their leaves. And when the corn ripened and he cooked it with his meat, he could once more taste the love and care she had always shown him. He understood then that his grandmother had kept her promise. Though she had gone from the Earth, she would always be with her people whenever they ate corn.

FOOD and food preparation are one way to say something about who we are as a group and how we relate to the rest of reality. Like the grandmother's corn in this Cherokee folktale, food is a chain that links the generations together. Specific foods say, "This is how we cook; this is how we eat; this is who we have been; and this is who we are."

Imagine how you would feel if you were all alone in a foreign country. The people speak a different language; they dress differently; they eat unfamiliar foods. You can't help but feel homesick and anxious. But then, as you're walking down the treet one day, you

The geographical region where we live and the ethnic group to which we belong are two of the factors that shapes our foodways. In 1869, an English traveler to America noted:

The Irish ate potatoes and the English did not.
The Irish put barley into their pot liquor [broth].
The English put in beans and had bean porridge.

Cod and corn are loved in New England. Sweet potatoes and grits (made from corn) are favorite foods in the South. Even the kind of bread we eat varies: Southerners like very soft bread; New Englanders prefer firm-textured bread; and Italians in New York City enjoy bread that is hard and crusty.

see up ahead familiar yellow arches—McDonald's!

No matter how you feel about fast food, if you found yourself in these circumstances, you would probably feel a rush of relief and comfort as you sank your teeth into a Big Mac. With time, if you found that other North Americans were visiting this same land, you might begin to meet together at McDonald's. Back home, you might not have thought you had all that much in common with these people, but now food would be the common link that bound you all together. You would no longer feel so alone.

The early settlers experienced something similar. As strangers in a strange land, immigrants to the New World found that food

FOOD AS A WAY OF REMEMBERING

Before Passover, many North American Jews join Jews around the world as they clear the house of all nonritual foods. During Passover, they eat particular foods that are vital aspects of this religious holiday. These foods are designed to call to mind the Jews' ancient exodus out of Egypt. Remembering their history through food and ritual affirms Jews' sense of their strong religious and cultural identity.

Preparing traditional foods like pizza allows us to feel close to our family and culture.

CROSSING THE MILES

When a family sends a "care package" of cookies and other home-baked goods to distant family members in college or the armed services, they are communicating: "Our love is still with you even though we are separated."

was a link to "home" that eased the shock of entering a new environment; what's more, it was a way to affirm their group identity, to say, "We are a group that belongs together."

The concept of fast food would have been completely strange to these early settlers, of course. In many cases case, food preparation was as important as the food itself, and these food traditions continue to be passed down through the generations.

Today, for instance, many Italian Americans still make sauce the way their mothers, grandmothers, and great-grandmothers made it back in Italy's small villages. They might be far away in terms of time and space, but each time they dribble the olive oil into the hot pan and fry the onion and garlic; each time they cut the tomatoes and put them in to simmer; each time they add a sprig of basil or a sprinkle of oregano, they reclaim their identity as links in a centuries-long chain of women.

These women make their memory of family and culture so real that passersby can smell it out in the street, and so tangible that the whole family can sit down and eat it. As one woman said, "When I breathed in the aroma of the sauce, it was like my grandmother's arms around my shoulders. And when we gathered around the table, each taste made me feel we were eating with a room full of friendly ghosts."

American Hindus use food to affirm their identity as well, but in their case, food links them to something even greater than family ties—an ancient religious tradition whose roots are far away in India. As they celebrate a daily afternoon meal called *prasadam*, they offer food to **Krishna**, the prime enjoyer and the prime provider. Believers eat this food not for them-

Joining hands around a table is a powerful expression of acceptance and welcome.

selves but for their god, and the foods themselves are thought to be Krishna's favorites—hot, spicy vegetarian dishes and very sweet desserts, using the ingredients of India. The entire experience is not only an act of worship but also a teaching tool to remind the entire group of who they are and what they believe.

Food's affirmation of membership in a particular group can be a positive experience; it demonstrates acceptance, inclusion, belonging. But unfortunately, the flip side of inclusion is exclusion. If we only allow a select few into our group, then we exclude all the rest.

Fear of newcomers in our midst may mean we also reject their **foodways**. After World War II, for example, American social workers tried to teach "nutrition" to African American and Italian immigrant families. Out of misguided kindness, the social workers hoped to erase that which made these groups "different." In a similar way, some early settlers separated meat into two categories: "fit to eat" and "Injun food."

European Americans once considered Chinese food unappetizing. Today it is a favorite food of nearly everyone.

FOOD AND RELIGION

Sometimes religion can shape the food we eat in purely practical ways. For instance, the strict Puritan ban against working on Sunday led to recipes that could be prepared the day before—and today, though few modern New Englanders' pattern their lives after Puritan theology, slow-baking brown bread and baked beans are still traditional favorites of the region.

According to sociologist Gordon Allport, familiarity gives human beings a sense of goodness, while strangeness gives a feeling of wrongness or evil. Those who look different, who have unfamiliar ways—and who eat differently as well—are often thought to be inferior or even dangerous, and their food is considered to be disgusting.

When this happens, foodways are no longer sources of positive identity; instead, they have become the foundation for **stereotypes**. Where a sense of identity honors reality's idiosyncrasies and individuality, stereotypes put reality in a box where it can barely breathe. Stereotypes all too often lead to prejudice, hatred, and even violence.

As human beings, all of us have a tendency to fear the unknown. But food has the power to communicate another powerful message: hospitality. Interestingly, both the words *hospitality* and *guest* come from the same word root, an ancient Latin word that meant *stranger* or *alien*. When we offer someone hospitality, we often give food to an honored guest—and by doing so, we

Day of the Dead celebrations affirm that even death cannot break the bonds between loved ones.

bring the stranger into our midst, so that they are alien no more. As we share a meal, we knock down the boundary lines that once separated us; we are no longer insiders and outsiders. Food draws us together into a new, united group.

This has happened across North America as cultural traditions learn to live with each other. Today we no longer look down on Italian and African American foods; instead, Italian and "soul food" restaurants thrive, as do other ethnic restaurants. We can see another parallel in the experience of Vietnamese immi-

TRADITIONAL HOSPITALITY

In Polish American homes the traditional greeting of "Guest in the house, God in the house," is always followed by the command to "Set another plate!" "Southern hospitality" also demands that the guest gets the best when it comes to food. One woman in the Northeast remembers that if food was short, her mother would whisper meaningfully, "FGE," which meant "Family go easy" to ensure that the "company" had plenty to eat.

Many cultures have made hospitality to strangers an important part of both their tradition and their daily life. A woman in the Pine Barrens of New Jersey recalls the way her family practiced hospitality:

> Everybody who came to the house had to eat something, regardless of whether it was meal time or not. It was customary to offer somebody something . . . because if they went away without eating, that was bad. There was always a piece of cake or pie, or perhaps a little chowder left on the stove. There was always something cooking.

From Brown, Linda Keller and Kay Mussell's *Ethnic and Regional Foodways in the United States* (Knoxville: University of Tennessee Press, 1984).

According to the New Testament Gospels, Christ ate a last meal with his friends before his death. Christians reenact this meal in the Communion ritual, affirming the ultimate victory of life over death.

grants when they first came to North America: urban folklore once blamed all missing cats and dogs on the newcomers, who were known to eat these animals as meat; today, however, Vietnamese restaurants are becoming popular additions to many communities. In yet another example, after the events of September 11, 2001, many mid-Eastern restaurants suffered, as stories circulated that the food was unclean; America's feelings about this particular kind of ethnic food were influenced by their fear of Islamic terrorists. As more and more Americans came to understand, however, that terrorism was their enemy rather than Islam itself, people once more began to enjoy the food offered by these cultures.

Food expresses our vision of who we are, as families, as cultures, as religions. But food also has the power to reach across

MEXICAN *PAN DE MUERTO* FOR DAY OF THE DEAD CELEBRATIONS (BREAD OF DEATH)

¼ cup margarine   2 tsps anise seed
¼ cup milk   ¼ cup sugar
¼ cup warm water   2 eggs, beaten
3 cups flour   ½ tsp salt
1¼ tsps active dry yeast   2 tsps orange zest (grated rind)

Combine ingredients and knead until dough is smooth. Let dough rise in a warm place until doubled in size (1–2 hours). Punch dough down and let rise again for about an hour, until nearly doubled in size. Use your fingers to mold the dough into the shapes of angels or animals. Bake at 350°F for 35 to 45 minutes. Let cool and brush with a glaze made from:

1 tbsp orange zest   ¼ cup sugar
¼ cup orange juice   2 tbsp sugar

Bring ingredients to a boil in a saucepan over medium heat and boil for two minutes. Brush glaze over the top of bread and sprinkle bread with sugar.

boundaries and pull us close. This power is so strong that it stretches over time and geographical distance.

In the folk traditions of many cultures, food can even reach beyond the greatest barrier of all—death. Mexican Americans, for instance, leave food on their loved ones' graves on the Day of the Dead. On the anniversary of a family member's death, Vietnamese Americans cook the person's favorite foods and place them on the household's altar to the ancestors. Italian immigrants once believed that the soul did not leave its earthly home until three days after death, and so families left a loaf of bread and a candle near an open door to nourish and illumine the departed one's journey. These food traditions say that death does not erase our membership in the human community. By extending food to the dead, the living community affirms the ongoing identity of those who have departed.

After a funeral, many cultures traditionally bring gifts of food to the remaining family. The entire community often gathers to feast, tying the group together as they nourish life in the face of death. Some folk traditions also call for special foods—the English have "soul cakes," Italians *fave dei morti* (beans of the dead), and Mexican Americans *pan de muerto* (bread of death). By eating these foods, the community symbolically consumes death, that which is most dangerous to our unity as human beings, even as it celebrates an ongoing union with loved ones who are gone.

In the situations we've discussed in this chapter, it would be hard to find a spoken or written word that means quite the same thing food does. No single word could express the same depth and power conveyed by a simple meal. Perhaps the words that come closest are these:

Life
Welcome.
Love.

The turkey has become the symbol of a North American food celebration—Thanksgiving.

SEVEN

Good Times
Food as Celebration

Thanksgiving Joys

The pilgrims and their traditional foods are important elements of American folklore.

I
N 1621, after a long hard year in the New World, the Puritans celebrated their first harvest with a feast. They shared their celebration with their Native American neighbors, and together the two groups sat down to tables groaning with food. Today we have transformed this feast of joy, plenty, and hospitality into Thanksgiving, one of North America's most important holidays. This celebration is rooted in the New World, and its traditions focus entirely on a particular set of foods—turkey, mashed potatoes and gravy, pumpkin pie. We do not give gifts at Thanksgiving; we do not have a prescribed religious ritual to attend; we have few songs to sing. We simply get together and eat (and eat . . . and eat!).

But food is also essential to our other important holidays. Those who celebrate Christmas cannot imagine the holiday without Christmas dinner—or cookies and eggnog. Fourth of July gatherings center on cookouts and picnic fare; Passover is rooted in an ancient meal; and many North Americans celebrate the end of Lent with Easter eggs and leg of lamb. Some North Americans even celebrate Super Bowl Sunday with chicken wings and pizza, food that can easily be eaten in living rooms in front of the television. Food is the focal point of more personal celebrations as well, like weddings, bar and bat mitzvahs, birthdays—which wouldn't be complete without the cake—and anniversary dinners. A salary raise, a new job, or news of a new baby on the way are all reasons to go out to dinner and enjoy special meals.

At gatherings like these, food expresses our joy. It even enhances events that might seem to have very little to do with food.

Edward Winslow, one of the early Puritan settlers at Plymouth, gave this account of the first Thanksgiving:

> Our harvest being gotten in, our governor sent four men on fowling, that so we might after a special manner rejoice together after we had gathered the fruit of our labors. They four in one day killed as much fowl as, with a little help beside, served the company almost a week. At which time, amongst other recreations, we exercised our arms. Many of the Indians coming amongst us, and among the rest their greatest King Massasoit, with some ninety men, whom for three days we entertained and feasted, and they went out and killed five deer, which they brought to the plantation and bestowed on our governor, and upon the captain and others.

From this we know that the feast went on for three days and included ninety Native Americans. Obviously, food was plentiful: in addition to the venison provided by the Indians, there was enough wild fowl to supply the village for a week. The fowl would have included ducks, geese, turkeys, and even swans.

Through the years, Thanksgiving has come to represent a nation's heritage of plenty.

For instance, what would a baseball game be without hotdogs . . . a movie without popcorn . . . a campout without marshmallows? Food makes the good times even better.

Life was hard for our ancestors, and food helped break the demanding tedium of their daily lives. Each season's special

FURMENTY

(A wheat pudding that may have been served at the first Thanksgiving in Plymouth.)

1 cup cracked wheat
¼ tsp. ground mace
1 quart milk
½ tsp. ground cinnamon
¾ cup milk
¼ cup brown sugar
½ cup heavy cream
2 egg yolks
½ tsp. salt
additional brown sugar

In a large pot, bring the water to a boil and add the wheat. Lower heat to simmer, cover, and continue to cook for a half hour, or until soft. Drain off all the water and add the milk, cream, salt, mace, cinnamon and sugar. Continue to simmer, stirring occasionally, until most of the liquid is absorbed (20 to 30 minutes). In a small bowl, beat the egg yolks and slowly stir ½ cup of the wheat mixture into the yolks. Then stir the yolk mixture into the pot, and continue cooking for another 5 minutes, stirring frequently. Serve sprinkled with brown sugar.

From Plimouth Plantation's *Thanksgiving Primer.*

THE HISTORY OF THANKSGIVING

After that first celebration, the Pilgrims did not hold Thanksgiving the next year, or any year thereafter, though some of their descendants later celebrated a "Forefather's Day" that usually occurred on December 21 or 22. Several presidents, including George Washington, ordered one-time Thanksgiving holidays that occurred at various times of the year. In 1827, Mrs. Sarah Josepha Hale began lobbying for Thanksgiving as a national holiday, but her efforts were unsuccessful until 1863, when Abraham Lincoln finally made it a national holiday.

In Canada, Thanksgiving is celebrated on the second Monday of October. The food traditions, however, are much the same as in the United States.

foods, each holiday feast, affirmed that despite the hardship, life was good. This tradition of celebration wove its way through folk stories and folk songs, and it continues today to be an essential element of North American culture.

North Americans love to eat. However, few of us today have the same physical demands that were put on our ancestors; we

A family Thanksgiving is a chance to celebrate life's goodness.

RECIPE FOR TURKEY STUFFING

2 quarts stale bread cubes
1 quart cornbread crumbs
1¼ cups chicken bouillon or stock
3 beaten eggs
1 cup butter or margarine
1 cup chopped onion

1 cup chopped parsley
1 tbsp salt
½ tsp pepper
2 cups chopped celery
1½ cups walnuts

Moisten bread cubes and cornbread crumbs with chicken bouillon or stock. Add beaten eggs to bread. Melt butter or margarine and simmer chopped onion in it for 1 minute. Add to bread mixture with parsley, salt, pepper, celery, and walnuts. Makes enough for a 12-pound turkey.

Vegetables were once the common fare of poor people, while only the wealthy ate much meat. In modern North America, though, people have to be reminded to eat their vegetables.

are no longer hardy settlers scraping out our livelihoods with grueling physical labor. As a result, many of us consume far more *calories* than we use—and obesity is a growing health problem in North America.

Food and eating is no longer so simple. At any given time, 90 percent of all American women and 50 percent of all Americans are trying to diet. For many, food has become a test of willpower, a matter for guilt.

Food folklore, however, reminds us of a simpler time. As we learn from our past, we can find new and healthy ways to live in the present. We may need to adjust our food traditions to better express today's reality—but rooted in these traditions, food still means joy . . . togetherness . . . and thanksgiving. Life has been good to us. We have reason to celebrate.

Let's eat!

Further Reading

Andrews, Tamra. *Nectar and Ambrosia: An Encyclopedia of Food in World Mythology*. Santa Barbara, Calif.: ABC-CLIO, 2000.

Brown, Linda Keller and Kay Mussell, eds. *Ethnic and Regional Foodways in the United States*. Knoxville: University of Tennessee Press, 1984.

Camp, Charles. *American Foodways: What, When, Why, and How We Eat in America*. Little Rock, Ark.: August House, 1989.

Miller, Joni. *American Cookbook*. New York: Harry N. Abrams, 1995.

Mints, Sidney. *Tasting Food, Tasting Freedom: Excursions into Eating, Culture, and the Past*. Boston: Beacon Press, 1996.

Nathan, Joan. *An American Folklife Cookbook*. New York: Schocken Books, 1984.

Wilson, David Scofield and Angus Kress Gillespie. *Rooted in America: Folklore of Popular Fruits and Vegetables*. Knoxville: University of Tennessee Press, 1999.

For More Information

American Folklore Society
afsnet.org

American Folk Kitchen
www.americanfolkkitchen.com

Food and Drink Lore
mythinglinks.org/ct~food.html

Food Folklore
www.ed.foods.com

Modern Food Folklore
nutrition.about.com

Glossary

Bayous Marshy areas.

Cajun A person in Louisiana descended from the French-speaking immigrants from Acadia in the north.

Calories The amount of heat required to raise the temperature of one kilogram of water one Celsius degree, used commonly for measuring food's ability to provide the body energy (that may be stored as fat if not needed).

Caribou A reindeer.

Communion The Christian religious ritual where participants reenact the Last Supper by symbolically eating the body and blood of Christ; also called the Eucharist.

Foodways Traditional customs involving food.

Krishna A Hindu god that preserves life; also called Vishnu in India.

Medieval Having to do with the Middle Ages, the period of European history from about A.D. 500 to 1500.

Phoenix A mythical bird that burns to death every 500 years and then rises to new life from its ashes.

Stereotypes Overly simple and often untrue mental pictures of certain groups of people.

Tamales A Mexican food; seasoned ground meat rolled in cornmeal dough, wrapped in cornhusks, and steamed.

Tortillas Mexican pancakes, made from either corn or wheat flour.

Index

Biographies

Ellyn Sanna has authored more than 50 books, including adult nonfiction, novels, young adult biographies, and gift books. She also works as a freelance editor and helps care for three children, a cat, a rabbit, a one-eyed hamster, two turtles, and a hermit crab.

Dr. Alan Jabbour is a folklorist who served as the founding director of the American Folklife Center at the Library of Congress from 1976 to 1999. Previously, he began the grant-giving program in folk arts at the National Endowment for the Arts (1974–76). A native of Jacksonville, Florida, he was trained at the University of Miami (B.A.) and Duke University (M.A., Ph.D.). A violinist from childhood on, he documented oldtime fiddling in the Upper South in the 1960s and 1970s. A specialist in instrumental folk music, he is known as a fiddler himself, an art he acquired directly from elderly fiddlers in North Carolina, Virginia, and West Virginia. He has taught folklore and folk music at UCLA and the University of Maryland and has published widely in the field.